MONKEEKEE'S GREAT ADVENTURE

CHARLIE WON

FANCY JUGGLING

Katie McGarry

Leny, the Juggling Bear

Friends Stick Together

Sharon Nao Kanes

HOORAY FOR BOOKS!

Words and pictures by

Brian Won

Houghton Mifflin Harcourt
Boston • New York

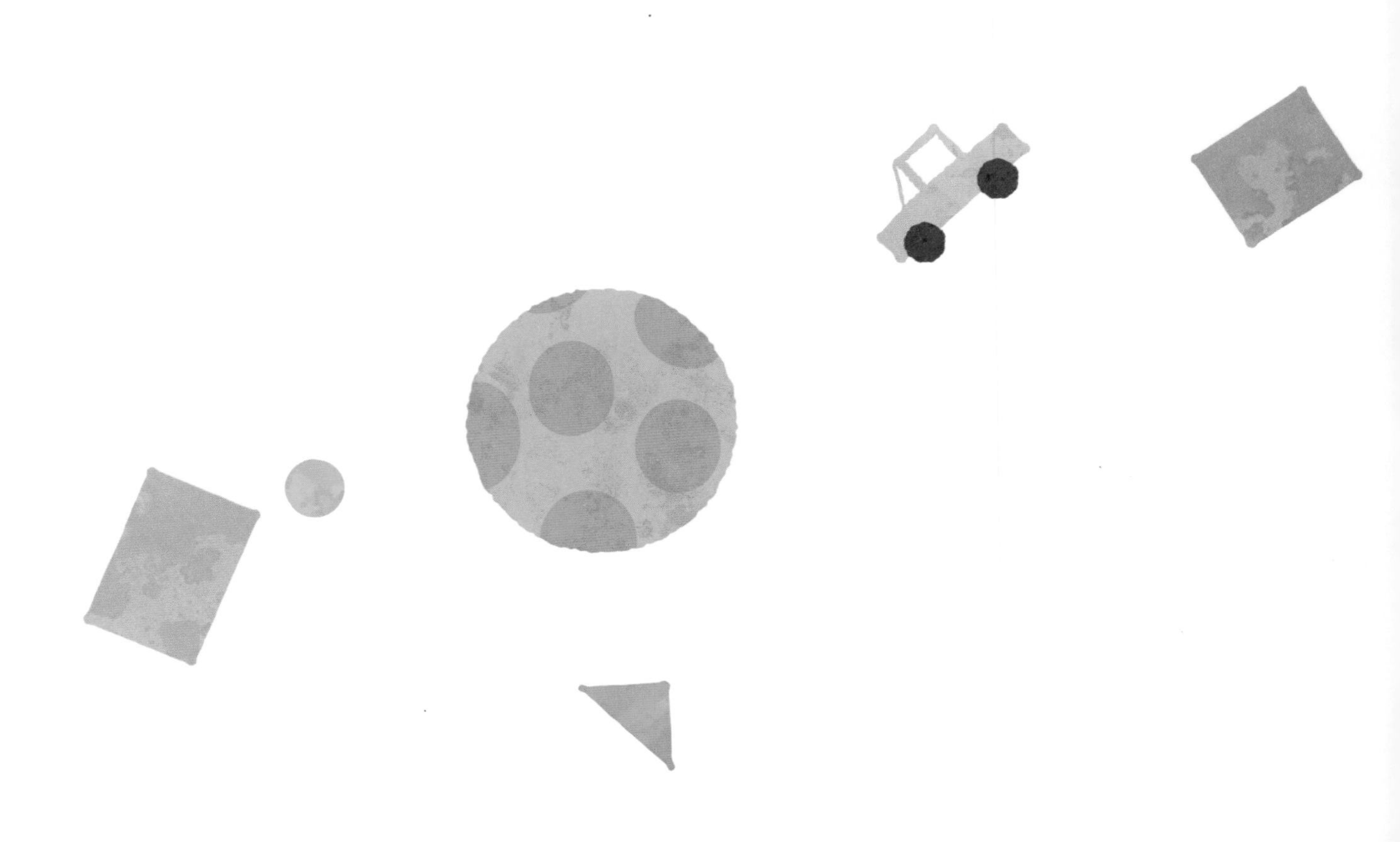

For Jeannette, for crossing every *t* and dotting every *i*

 For information about permission to reproduce selections from this book, write to trade.permissions@hmhco.com or to Permissions, Houghton Mifflin Harcourt Publishing Company, 3 Park Avenue, 19th Floor, New York, New York 10016. • www.hmhco.com • The text type was set in Neutra Text. The display type was set in Trade Gothic. • Library of Congress Cataloging-in-Publication Data is available. • ISBN: 978-0-544-74802-6 • Manufactured in China • SCP 10 9 8 7 6 5 4 3 2 1
4500657927

"Where is that book?
It's my favorite!" Turtle said.
He searched his entire house—
but no book.

HOORAY!

"Where could it be?" Turtle wondered.

"Aha! Maybe I shared it with . . .

. . . Zebra! I hope he liked it. I can't wait to read it again.

RAY

FOR BOOKS!"

But Zebra did not have Turtle's book anymore.

"Why don't you read these

two favorites of mine?" said Zebra.

"They are about unicorns!"

But Turtle said,

"I LIKE MY BOOK!

Maybe you shared it with . . .

. . . Owl! Let's go see."

Turtle and Zebra cheered,

"HOORAY FOR BOOKS!"

But Owl did not have Turtle's book anymore.

"It was a great book, but check out
some of mine instead," Owl said.
"This one is about eagles."

But Turtle said,

"I LIKE **MY** BOOK!

Maybe you shared it with . . .

The Magical Unicorn

. . . Giraffe! Let's go check."

Turtle and Zebra and Owl cheered,

"HOORAY
FOR BOOKS!"

But Giraffe did not have Turtle's book anymore.

"I did enjoy it," said Giraffe.

"Now, how about these?

I love this one about roller skating!"

But Turtle said,

"I LIKE MY BOOK!

Maybe you shared it with . . .

LET'S ROLLER SKATE!

. . . Elephant! Let's go get it."

They all cheered,

"HOORAY FOR BOOKS!"

"I sure hope we find my favorite,"

Turtle said.

Juggling
JUGGLIN'

But Elephant did not have Turtle's book anymore.

"It was a very good story," Elephant said.

"Now I can share these with you.

Here's one about juggling!"

But Turtle said,

"I LIKE **MY** BOOK!

Did you share it with . . .

JUGGLIN'
FANCY JUGGLING
JUGGLE

. . . Lion? There it is! I see it! There's my favorite!"

Turtle reached for the very last book on the bottom of Lion's giant pile and yanked hard.

"Thank you, Lion!"

FANCY JUGGLING
JUGGLIN'
LENY

Turtle cheered, "I finally found my favorite!

HOORAY FOR BOOKS!"

FRIENDS
4
EVER

Turtle found a place all to himself.

It was very quiet.

He read his book once,

then twice,

then three times.

LET'S ROLLER SKATE!
THE FLYING TURTLE

Then Turtle heard Elephant say,
"My book is so funny!"
Zebra said, "This book is so sad."
Owl said, "Giraffe, you should read this story!"
Lion added, "I bet Turtle would love this one."

LENY
LET'S
ROLLER
SKATE!

Turtle came closer. He asked,
"Who wants to read my favorite book again?
It's about friends!
Will you share your favorites with me?"
And everyone cheered, "Let's read together!"

“HOORAY FOR STORY TIME!”

FRIENDS
4 EVER!!

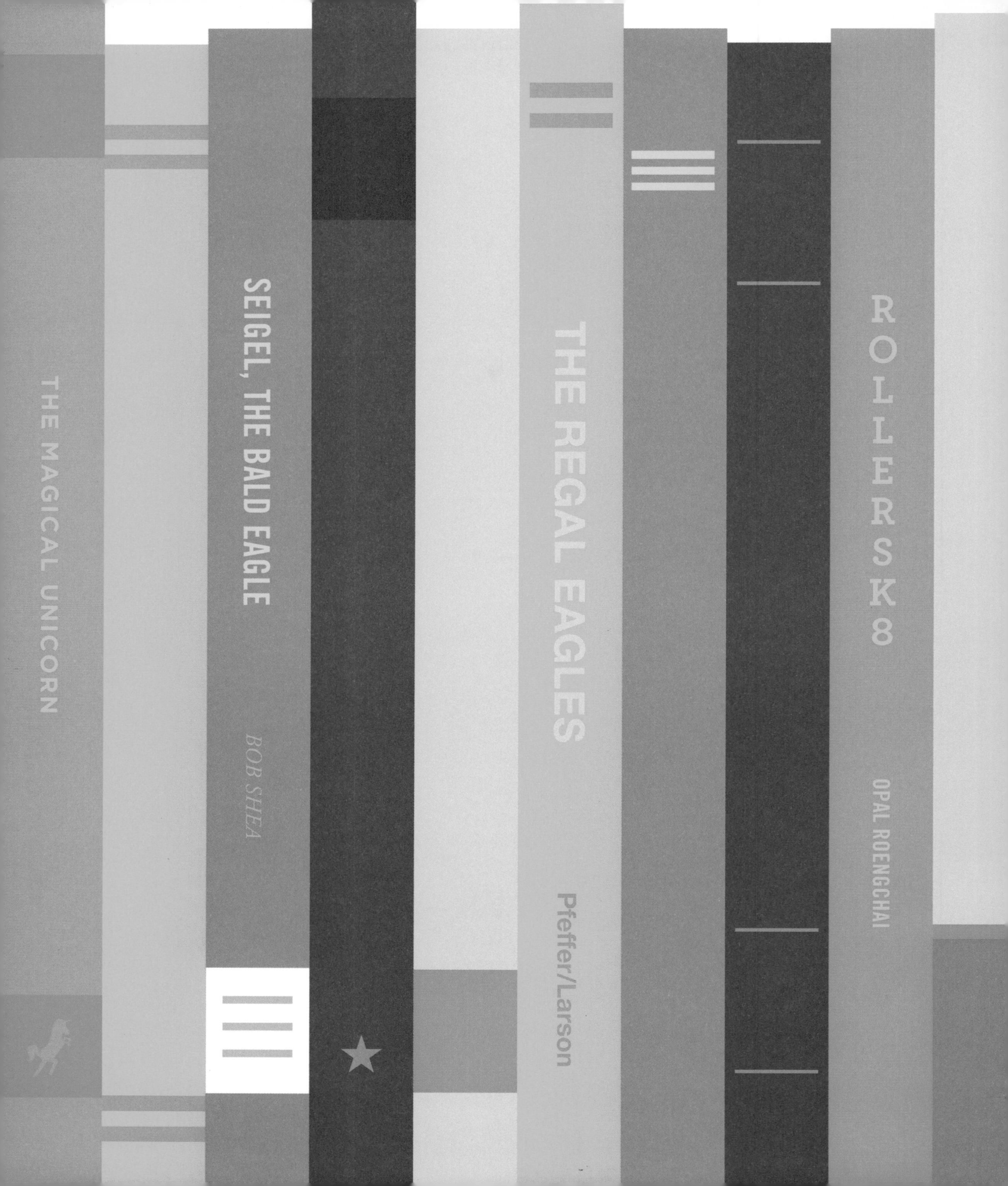

THE MAGICAL UNICORN

SEIGEL, THE BALD EAGLE

BOB SHEA

THE REGAL EAGLES

Pfeffer/Larson

ROLLERSK8

OPAL ROENGCHAI